KU-216-737

For Lucia

A TEMPLAR BOOK

First published in the UK in 2009 by Templar Publishing,
an imprint of The Templar Company Limited,
The Granary, North Street, Dorking, Surrey, RH41DN, UK
www.templarco.co.uk

Copyright © 2009 by Thomas Docherty

www.thomasdocherty.co.uk

First edition

All rights reserved

ISBN 978-1-84011-423-2

Printed in China

Thomas Docherty

BIG SCARY MONSTER

templar publishing

On top of a mountain, not very far from here, there once lived a Big Scary Monster.

This monster was bigger and scarier than any other creature – and he knew it.

All the other little creatures that lived on the mountain spent their days playing happily together among the small rocks and small plants.

But suddenly, when they least expected it,
something disturbed the peace...

As time went by, the little creatures learned to hide from the Big Scary Monster. He soon got bored because he couldn't find anyone to scare.

One day, he stood at the top of the mountain and looked down into the valley. Far below, the Big Scary Monster saw many more little creatures playing happily among the small rocks and small plants.

'I'll go down there and scare them as well,' he thought to himself.

So off he went down the mountain.

But as he walked, a strange thing happened.

The further he went, the larger the things around him seemed to grow.

The small rocks...

became big rocks.

The small plants...

became big plants.

And the little creatures that
had seemed so small from the top of the mountain...

were actually very, very big.

The Big Scary Monster had never
felt so small and scared in his life.
He looked for somewhere to hide.

'I wish I was back on the top of the mountain with the little creatures and the small rocks and small plants,' thought the Big Scary Monster to himself.

But suddenly, when he least expected it...

Back up the mountain ran the Big Scary Monster.

The big plants...

became small plants.

The big rocks...

became small rocks.

And the little creatures...

were nowhere to be found.

The Big Scary Monster felt so alone that he sat down
and started to cry.

Then suddenly, when he least expected it...

BOO!

The Big Scary Monster was so pleased to see the little creatures that he forgot all about being big and scary.

From that day forward, everyone became friends and played happily together at the top of the mountain. And can you guess what their favourite game was?